Bubbles
the dwarf zebu

A Story About Finding a Home at the Saint Louis Zoo

Written and illustrated by Carolyn Mueller

REEDY PRESS
St. Louis, Missouri

Once upon a time, but not very long ago,
a beautiful young cow lived in the land of india.

She was a special kind of cow, a proud cow.
Her great-great-great-many-many-more-greats-
grandmother was the first cow in india.

They called this little cow a dwarf zebu.

The dwarf zebu loved india. The sun was warm, the food was spicy, and everywhere she looked there were bright colors.

The Indian people were the best of all. They loved the little dwarf zebu! They treated her like a *shehzadi* . . . a princess!

To the people in india, the little dwarf zebu represented all that is good about life. She gave them so much, and they respected her for it. She used all of her energy, pulling their plows and carts every day.

The people in 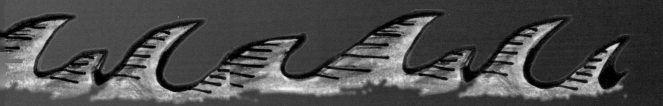 india were happy. And the little dwarf zebu was happy. Because everyone loved her so much, they chose the little zebu for a special journey.

She was going to cross the big, blue ocean to live in a new home . . . the USA!

The little dwarf zebu saw the sun rise and set many times on her journey until she finally, **FINALLY**, made it to **AMERICA.**

She was sent to live on a farm. Other cattle lived on the farm too. But these cattle did not look like the little zebu.

They did not have silvery grey coats.

They had
spots.

They were quite different from the zebu.

"What is that funny flap on your neck?" one cow asked.

"Look at your silly hump!" another cow said.

The dwarf zebu was sad. She missed the bright colors and spices of india. She was embarrassed by her flap and her hump.

The farmer saw that the little zebu was lonely and sent her to a happier place to live . . . the

SAINT LOUIS ZOO!

She had a cozy barn and a nice yard at the Zoo. She had wonderful neighbors—two friendly otters and a group of wooly sheep!

Just like in india, at the Zoo she could stand in the warm sun and watch all of the children dressed in bright colors as they went by.

The little zebu's favorite thing to do was watch her otter friends blow bubbles in their pool. Because she loved this so much, everyone at the Zoo started calling her "Bubbles."

Bubbles was happy in her new home. Then one day, a new friend came to live in her yard. The new friend, Xavier, a goat, had white and black spots. To Bubbles, he looked just like the mean cows.

Bubbles was worried that Xavier would tease her about her flap and her hump just as the cows had.

"I am a goat," said Xavier.

"I am a cow," said Bubbles.

"You don't look like the cows I know," said Xavier.
"You have a flap and a hump."

"Yes," said Bubbles, shyly. "I am a special kind of cow.
I am called a dwarf zebu. All zebus have **flaps**. We call
them dewlaps. All zebus have **humps**. We can live off of
the fat inside our humps for days and days."

"That is neat," said Xavier. "See, I don't have a hump,
but I've got these little **hooves** to help me climb!"

"That is special too," said Bubbles.

And they smiled.

Every day Bubbles and Xavier played together.

They ate hay together.

They stood in the sunshine together.

And they watched all of the bright colors and children go by.

Bubbles is a long way from india.

But do you know what?

She is still treated like a *shehzadi* . . . a princess.

ABOUT THE DWARF ZEBU

A dwarf zebu is a type of cattle originating from the zebu cattle of India. Zebu are one of the oldest known breeds of cattle. They are easily recognized by their silvery grey coats, the distinctive humps on their withers (known as dewlaps), and the flaps of skin under their necks. If food and water are limited, a dwarf zebu can live off of the fat and muscle stored in the hump.

Dwarf zebu like warm weather. Zebu cattle are not raised for meat or milk. They make excellent draft animals and are often used to pull plows and carts in India. There are more than 200 million zebu in India. They provide more power than all of the Indian electric plants combined!

The zebu is considered a sacred cow in India.

AT THE SAINT LOUIS ZOO!

The real-life Bubbles can be found in the Emerson Children's Zoo at the Saint Louis Zoo. The Zoo was founded in 1910, and throughout its history, Zoo employees have worked hard to care for animals and wildlife.

The Saint Louis Zoo's mission is to conserve animals and their habitats through animal management, research, recreation, and educational programs that encourage, support, and enrich the experience of the public.

Zoos that are currently accredited by the Association of Zoos and Aquariums work to give animals naturalistic environments, healthy diets, and plenty of training and enrichment. Through positive reinforcement training, animals are provided challenges and rewards.

frog pond

alpacas

tunnel

cz building

bubblers

playground

otters

bubbles!

Using enrichment, zookeepers can create surroundings that encourage natural behaviors, give each animal control over his or her environment, and provide physical and mental stimulation.

Many zoos are also focused on conserving wildlife and habitats. For example, the Saint Louis Zoo WildCare Institute is dedicated to creating a sustainable future for wildlife and for people around the world.

Visit Bubbles and her friends at the Saint Louis Zoo to learn more about endangered species and what you can do to help!

In memory of Nana.
Artist, writer, and friend to all creatures, I owe my inspiration to you. Toot toot!

And to all those who work every day of the year through heat, ice, dirt, dust, mud, feathers, and claws to take care of each and every special animal at the Saint Louis Zoo. I am sure that Bubbles, and all of her friends, appreciate the love.

Reedy Press
PO Box 5131
St. Louis, MO 63139, USA

No part of this publication may be reproduced or transmitted in any form or by any means, electronic or mechanical, including photocopy, recording, or any information storage and retrieval system, without permission in writing from the publisher.

Permissions may be sought directly from Reedy Press at the above mailing address or via our website at www.reedypress.com.

Library of Congress Control Number: 2012933959

ISBN: 978-1-935806-29-5

Please visit our website at www.reedypress.com.

Endsheet photographs by Katie Twellman and Carolyn Mueller

Printed in the United States of America
12 13 14 15 16   5 4 3 2 1